FOURTEEN RATS & A RAT~CATCHER

TAMASIN COLE
story by James Cressey

Prentice-Hall, Inc.

Englewood Cliffs, New Jersey

Once upon a time, long long ago, a nice old lady lived in a cottage in the forest.
But she had a nasty family of rats under her floor.

First American edition published 1977 by
Prentice-Hall, Inc., Englewood Cliffs, New Jersey

10   9   8   7   6   5   4   3   2   1

Library of Congress Cataloging in Publication Data

Cressey, James.
    Fourteen rats & a rat-catcher.

    SUMMARY: A little old lady with a house full of rats
calls on the town rat catcher who does more than solve
her rat problem.
    [1. Rats—Fiction]   I. Cole, Tamasin.   II. Title.
PZ7.C8643Fo3   [E]   77-4759
ISBN 0-13-329920-1

Printed in Great Britain

Once upon a time, long long ago, a nice rat family lived under the floor of a tiny cottage in the forest. But they had a nasty old lady living above them.

One day the old lady went into town
to do her shopping.
She went into a small pet shop.

'Good riddance!' shouted the happy rats.
'Now we have our home to ourselves!'
So they ran riot about the cottage.

That evening the old lady came back with a cat—
a very handsome cat, a very large cat.

'Deary me,' said the rats when they saw the cat.
'What a vicious looking cat and how very ugly!'

So the old lady and her friendly pet
tried to catch the horrible rats.
Without any luck at all.

The rats were very nimble and,
with a great deal of luck,
avoided the wicked old lady and her pest.

At the end of a week, when the handsome cat
hadn't caught a single rat,
the old lady took him back to town in disgrace.

'Good riddance!' shouted the happy rats,
and they celebrated with tea and buttered biscuits.

That evening the old lady came back
with an old man—the town's rat-catcher.
He was a very pleasant old man,
a very handsome old man.

'Deary me,' said the rats
when they saw the rat-catcher.
'What a horrid old man and how very ugly!'

The old lady and the rat-catcher
had a nice cup of tea together
and took a real liking to each other.

While the unhappy rat family—
without any appetite at all—
looked on and hated both of them.

That night the rat-catcher sat down and plotted how to get rid of the rats.

While the rats put their noses together and plotted how to get rid of the rat-catcher.

The rat-catcher went out into the barn
looking for the rats.

And the largest rat went out into the barn, looking for the rat-catcher.

The rat-catcher and the largest rat met and plotted together.

Upstairs the old lady lay asleep dreaming, about the rats and the rat-catcher.

In the morning when the old lady came downstairs there wasn't a rat to be seen.
Just the nice rat-catcher.

While under the floor the rats kept very very quiet.

So the nice old lady married
the handsome old rat-catcher.

And the rats were happy
because the rat-catcher had promised
not to catch them—
if they kept quiet, as quiet as mice.